I072009

SEE YOU WHEN THE WORLD ENDS

by

SIMON PAUL WILSON

for all the readers and dreamers

SEE YOU WHEN THE WORLD ENDS

25

"So answer me this, what would you do if you found out the world was going to end?"

Naomi Wong lights yet another cigarette and inhales deeply.

"Depends on how much time we're talking about," she replies after blowing a smoke ring. "I mean, are we talking years, months, or hours here?"

"Hours," I say, "maybe less."

"That's easy then. I would find the nearest cute guy and screw his brains out."

"Really? That's how you would spend your final hour on Earth? Humping a complete stranger?"

"Yep."

"What if you couldn't find a cute enough guy? What if it's all fat, middle-aged businessmen as far as the eye can see?"

"Then I'd find a hot girl."

"Really?"

"Yep."

"Damn, I wish we only had one hour left to live."

Naomi laughs and launches another smoke ring into the air.

"Don't get too excited, smart-ass. If we *did* only have an hour left to live, I wouldn't be performing a girl-on-girl show for *your* benefit."

"Life's a bitch," I say.

"Sure is," says Naomi.

We lie in silence for a while and gaze up at an ocean of stars.

This is how we often spend our free evenings, if the weather is good enough. We lie in my back garden, drink a few beers and ask each other inane questions. This evening's first debate topic was whether either of us would be willing to have a little finger amputated for a large sum of money. I said yes, she said no.

Naomi sits up and hugs her knees to her chest.

"What about you?" she asks. "What would you do?"

I close my eyes and let out a long, deep sigh.

"I'd probably lie here and watch the stars go out."

"Kind of depressing, don't you think?"

I open my eyes to see Naomi flick her cigarette butt away . It glides through the air in a perfect arc before hitting the fence in a shower of red and yellow sparks.

"It wouldn't be that depressing if you were here," I say.

Naomi reaches for her beer and drains what is left.

"You say the sweetest things," she says, tossing the can over her shoulder. "But I'm afraid I'll be busy that night."

I laugh and join her in an upright position.

"Yeah, I forgot about that," I lie.

"You're so full of shit. I *know* you're thinking about it."

I do my best to suppress a guilty smile. Naomi looks up at the sky and says, "I know *I* am."

With that, we howl at the moon like the lunatics we are.

I met Naomi Wong about a year and a half ago. Her boyfriend at the time was a good friend of mine called Stephen. The three of us used to hang out with a whole bunch of other people from university and spent our weekends drinking too much and talking utter nonsense in very loud voices.

After seeing each other for six months, Stephen and Naomi drifted apart and we watched as their relationship petered out. There were no fights or arguments, no fireworks or shock revelations; one day they were an item and the next they weren't.

Although their separation was kind of mutual, the aftershock rocked our little group to the core and screwed up the whole dynamic. Some people found it difficult to judge where their loyalties lay and our usually raucous conversations became stilted and awkward when Stephen and Naomi were both present. It wasn't long until our group began to splinter and our weekend antics were a thing of the past.

Naomi and I continued to see each other however and formed our own merry band of two. There is no romance involved. Our friendship is based purely on a shared love of music, books and odd lines of conversation. A lot of people find this hard to believe, but it's true. We are good friends and that's as far as it goes.

We move from my back garden into my kitchen. We sit in silence, me staring at my coffee while Naomi continues to smoke herself to an early grave. I take a big gulp of cold coffee and wince at the bitterness. Naomi stubs out her cigarette in the overflowing ashtray and looks at her watch.

"I suppose I better be going," she says.

"I suppose so," I say. "What time do you have to check in?"

Naomi lowers her head to the table and groans, weakly holding up four fingers and her thumb.

"Good job you're an early riser then." I laugh.

"Fuck off," she replies, reducing her finger count and tucking her thumb in.

"Charming."

"Aren't I just?"

She lifts her head from the table and sits up. After tucking a loose strand of hair behind her right ear, she jams another cigarette between her lips.

"One for the road." She winks, lighting up.

I put the kettle on for another cup of instant and tell her it sucks she will be away until the start of the next term.

Naomi nods.

"Yeah, but it isn't every day your sister gets married, is it?"

"I guess not," I reply. "But it's going to be weird not having you around."

"Aw, poor lamb," she mocks with a smile. "You going to miss me?"

"Like a hole in the head."

I pour hot water into my mug and return to the table.

"So what's your sister like?" I ask.

"Just like me," she says, grinding her cigarette out and knocking a pile of ash onto the table. "But not as weird."

"Nobody could be as weird as you."

"That's true."

Naomi brushes the small ash mountain from the table and into her empty coffee mug.

"Is she as messy as you?"

We wait at my front garden gate for Naomi's taxi to arrive. I look up to see the stars have all but disappeared; the moon has also been obscured by clouds. I think of the end of the world and hope for a clear night sky.

"How do you think it will end?" I ask. "What form will the apocalypse take?"

"My money is on a meteor."

"Not zombies?"

"Zombies are an option, but I'm gonna go with a huge meteor."

"Let's see who's right," I say. "The winner gets to buy dinner."

"If we survive, idiot."

"Sure we'll survive," I tell her. "Me and you are born survivors."

"What if it happens while I'm in Hong Kong? We'll be on the other side of the world to each other!"

"Well, in the case of a zombie plague, I'll have to make my way to Hong Kong to meet you. If a meteor hits the Earth, you'll have to find your way back here."

"Sounds fair enough to me," Naomi says, offering me

her right hand to shake. "You got yourself a deal, partner."

Our handshake turns into a hug as the taxi pulls up next to us. Our embrace feels more like that of lovers than friends. We separate awkwardly, both of us wearing embarrassed smiles.

"Take care," I say.

She sticks her tongue out at me, opens the door of the taxi and dives inside. I close the door behind her. Something inside my heart fractures as I realise how empty my days will be without her.

As the taxi starts to pull off, Naomi opens the window and shouts, "See you when the world ends."

I wave and watch the cab's rear lights grow smaller, fade and disappear.

24

Naomi calls me at four thirty the following morning.

"I've checked in," she says.

"Wonderful," I croak. "What time is it?"

"Half past four. Did I wake you up?"

"Yes."

"Cool."

"I'm glad you think so."

The background hubbub of the airport increases in volume. Naomi follows suit and threatens to damage my eardrums permanently.

"I'M HAVING A SMOKE OUTSIDE. THERE

ARE NO SMOKING ROOMS HERE! HOW THE HELL ARE PEOPLE EXPECTED TO GO THAT LONG WITHOUT NICOTINE? IT'S FUCKING RIDICULOUS!"

"I'm sure you'll survive."

"THAT'S NOT THE POINT, STUPID."

"Please tell me why I'm going to miss you exactly."

"BECAUSE I'M AWESOME."

"That's what you think."

"THAT'S WHAT I KNOW! ANYWAY, GOTTA GO. EMAIL YOU LATER. BYE."

I say goodbye but she has already ended the call. I close my eyes and attempt to return to my slumber. Sadly, the damage has been done; I am now awake. Thank you, Naomi.

At nine o'clock, I receive another phone call. This time it's from my parents to inform me they are alive and well and enjoying their holiday.

"Hello from Thailand!" my father says. I can hear a slight quiver of excitement in his voice and feel a pang of jealousy.

"Hello from home," I reply. "How was the flight?"

"Not bad. The seats were comfortable, plenty of legroom, for a change. The flight attendants were *very* beautiful ..."

"What's the hotel like?" I ask before my father can get into trouble.

"Oh, it's amazing. You can see the whole of the city from our window. I took some photos last night, I'll send you them later.

Do you want a quick word with your mum?"

Before I can reply, the phone has been passed over and my mother continues the conversation.

"You would love it here. It really is wonderful and *so* cheap! Our hotel is like a palace and it didn't cost a lot. Oh, and the people are *so* friendly. You really should have come with us you know."

"Maybe I should have," I admit.

"Well, we have to go now. I bet this phone call is costing an arm and a leg. We will give you a call when we get to Singapore."

"Fine, look after yourself and have a good time."

"We will. Are you OK? How are things at home?"

I reply that I'm good and start to tell her about Naomi returning to Hong Kong.

"Sorry, we have to go," my mother interrupts. "I think we're almost out of credit. Talk later. Love you. Bye."

I slump down on the sofa and ask myself why everyone I know is leaving me and heading for Asia.

It's now ten in the morning and, by my calculations, Naomi will have been on the plane for about three hours, so there is no point in checking my email. Instead, I make my way around the house and clear up her trail of devastation from last night.

As I retrieve the last of the cigarette butts and beer cans from the garden, I feel like I am erasing all evidence of her ever having been here. By the time I have cleaned the kitchen and emptied the ashtray and cups, it is as though the events of last night never took place. This saddens me a little.

I resume my place on the sofa and stare at the magnolia ceiling. It is either this or sit in front of my computer, waiting for an email to arrive from Hong Kong. I notice a slight crack in the ceiling and trace its path from the light fitting to the left hand corner of the room.

When did my life lose all sense of purpose?

I close my eyes and resolve to find something, anything, to fit the yawning chasm Naomi has left behind.

All I find is sleep.

I awake from a dream, the details of which start to fade the second my eyes open. By the time I get up from the sofa, the dream has been almost entirely wiped from my memory. The only thing I can remember is a mirror, but I can't even be sure of that.

I've never been able to recall my dreams, no matter how vivid they were. As soon as I'm awake, my mind sees my dreams as junk mail and promptly deletes them. I often feel envious of Naomi as she has total recall. Some of her dreams translate into stories that can last well over an hour. I guess some people are born dreamers.

Midnight approaches and I realise I've done little else except think about what I should do with myself now Naomi has left.

Avoiding the temptation to switch on my computer, I take a shower instead.

I stand in front of the bathroom mirror and take a good long look at myself. The person in the mirror gives me a half-hearted smile. I tell him he needs to buck up his ideas and get a life, not pine away because his best friend has gone for a month or so.

He nods back at me and says that will be the first thing he'll do tomorrow morning, as soon as he has checked his mail.

I tell him he's being pathetic.

He agrees and says so am I.

Damn him for being right.

23

FROM: Naomi
TO: Tim
SUBJECT: Naomi hits HK!

Hey,
Well, here I am back home in HK and I have to say it sucks. Dad doesn't know I smoke, so now I have to visit the shops about five times a day so I can have as many smokes as possible before going back home with a tube of toothpaste or something.

I'm also now becoming addicted to mints, as I have to eat about twenty of the damn things to hide the smell of smoke. My dad must think I'm some sort of dental hygiene freak as I always smell minty fresh. Haha.

The flight was a bloody nightmare!
The guy behind me kept kicking the back of my chair for the entire journey and the people in front of me had a baby with them who just screamed and screamed and screamed. I swear that kid must have had lungs the size of an elephant. She was damn cute though, bless her. Then when I got to the airport, I stood at the wrong baggage carousel for twenty minutes. What an idiot! I really shouldn't be allowed to fly by myself. I'm a complete disaster at times, as you well know. Hehe.

Weather here is fucking hot! I'd forgotten how humid HK can be. I hate to say this, but now I totally prefer English summers with their highs of about twenty-five degrees. Thank fuck for air-con is all I can say.

My sister is going nuts at the minute. I swear she must think she's the only person who's ever got married. If she makes it to the wedding without having a heart attack, it will be a miracle.
At the moment, I'm trying to twist her arm into going out with me so I can get her drunk.
Yes, I'm totally going to corrupt my sister.
Actually, that's not true. Fact is my sister corrupted me. She was a real crazy girl, back before she became Little Miss

Prim and Proper. All I want is for her to let her hair down and go back to being the wild child I used to look up to, even if it's just for one night.

The one thing that's completely doing my head in is that my mum is now asking when I'm gonna get married.
For fucks sake!
Can you imagine that?
Me?
Married???
The thought scares the hell out of me. For a start, who in their right mind would take me on? Hahahaha!

I was thinking of maybe taking a short holiday after all this wedding madness has finished. I think I'll need it. Perhaps I'll go to Thailand for a few days or so. Your mum and dad are over there, right? Maybe I could meet up with them and tell them about all your bad habits!
Only joking. Everyone knows you are an angel and it's me who uses the dark side of the force.

Anyway, I'm gonna say bye now cause my head is all fuzzy because of the jetlag and all that. I'll email you again later.

Don't miss me too much, you hear? Hahaha!

Bye for now,

N.

22

FROM: Tim
TO: Naomi
SUBJECT: Tim is bored.

Hey you,
Glad to hear you managed to get home safely.
I have to be honest and say that receiving your email has
got to be the single most exciting thing to happen since you
left.

Yes, my life really is that dull.

Funny you should mention my parents, they called the other day to tell me just how wonderful Thailand is. I now regret not joining them on their trip around Asia. More fool me for thinking having the house to myself for three weeks would be the better option.
Oh well, you live and learn.

Your sister corrupted *you*? I find that very difficult to believe.
Try not to be so hard on her for going a little nuts. I think most brides-to-be get really stressed out the closer it gets to the big day.
I remember when my cousin was getting married. She was definitely not fun to be around.

Maybe a night out on the tiles is a good idea. Just try not to go too crazy! Remember you want your sister to enjoy herself, right?
Feeling like death and hugging the toilet for most of the night is not really that much fun. You of all people should know this. Do I need to show you the photos again?
Yeah, I'm being Mister Sensible here, but you know I'm right.

On another sensible note, perhaps this is a good time for you to ditch the cigarettes and just stick with the mints. What do you think?
For a start, mints are much cheaper, don't lead to terminal

diseases and smelling minty-fresh is no bad thing.
Plus, if you were to pack in the smokes, I wouldn't have to spend hours collecting up all your cigarette ends from my back garden.
Perhaps I may have exaggerated there a little about it taking hours, but all the same ...

OK, I will get off my soapbox now and finish my anti-smoking lecture.
You know it's only because I care, right?

Right, I'll bring this email to a close, as I've decided I need to get out of the house and try to do something with my time.
I'm not exactly sure what I'll do, but the point here is to try and do something other than watch movies or stare at my monitor.
I'm thinking of heading into the city, perhaps having lunch and maybe looking for some new music or a book or two.
Not the most exciting of days, granted, but at the very least, it may give me something to write to you about.

Give my best wishes to your sister, have fun and try to stay out of trouble!

Speak to you soon,

Tim.

21

I am officially lost without Naomi Wong.

After spending three hours wandering around the city center and its countless shops, I still haven't managed to buy a single thing. If Naomi were here, my wallet would now be nigh on empty and the two of us would be on our way to a restaurant or café to refuel, examine our purchases and consider whether we should put dents in our credit cards.

Do I really need her *that* much? Am I now incapable of choosing a book or a movie or some music without her assistance?

I march back into a nearby music store, determined to prove that choosing a CD on my own is not beyond me. After scouring the racks for almost an hour, I finally choose two from the sale section. I join the queue to pay and do my best to ignore the fact that both CDs are by artists Naomi likes. I hand my choices over to a girl at the counter who comments on my good taste in music.

"Oh, thanks," I say with a smile.

"I love Ladytron," she says. "Have you seen them in concert?"

"Yeah," I say. "They're fantastic live."

"How the hell would you know?" says a voice inside. *"You've never seen them live! That was Naomi! Why are you lying?"*

I want to tell the voice to shut the fuck up, but he is absolutely right. I pay the smiling sales assistant and leave before my nose grows or something.

On the opposite side of the street is a bookshop, providing me with a second chance to prove I still possess an opinion of my own. I leap at the opportunity to redeem myself and enter the store without further delay, resolved to finding something that isn't somehow connected to a certain girl in Hong Kong.

Instead of ambling aimlessly around the shop, I head straight to the new releases in the hope of discovering something. Sadly, most of them are not to my taste. My teenage years are behind me and I have no passion for supernatural romance. Many of the other books on display fall into the self-help category. Not my cup of tea either, but one of them catches my eye. I take a copy of the book from the shelf to take a closer look. The cover depicts an attractive girl with eyes closed, her content smile suggests she's sleeping peacefully.

Say Goodbye to Bad Dreams by Aurora.
That's her name? Just 'Aurora'? No surname or anything?
"That's a great book," says a voice. "I totally recommend it."
The owner of the voice is a blonde girl in shades who is so thin she looks ill. The phrase 'I have seen more meat on a pencil' would sum her up perfectly.
"Aurora's a great writer," she beams. "I've read all of her stuff. She's really helped me a lot."
This girl has a lovely smile, but I can't stop thinking about how skeletal she is. Part of me wants to invite this book-recommending stranger for lunch, possibly dinner too, so I can help bring her back from the brink of death.
"Have you read any of her books?" she asks.
"No, I haven't. The cover just took my eye, so …"
"Do you have trouble sleeping? Nightmares?" she asks, her head cocked to one side.
"No. Actually, if anything, I have trouble remembering dreams."
"Well, that's not the book for you," she says cheerily. "Come with me, I'll show you a good one to start with."
She walks off into the store without looking back to check if I am following. I walk after her. I have nothing better to do and this may give me something to write to Naomi about. The girl leads me upstairs and towards the self-help section. Only when she stops does she finally turn to see if I am still with her. When she sees I am, she gives me another flash of her cute smile.
"All of her books are here," she says. "I would recommend this one, seeing as you have trouble with

dream recall."

She reaches up for a book, takes it from the shelf and presents it to me as if it were made of gold. I take the offering and give the cover a once over. The book is called 'Dream Recall', go figure, and features the same model as her other book.

"Is this Aurora?" I ask.

The girl shakes her head.

"Nope, Aurora is Japanese."

The girl offers me her hand to shake.

"I'm Abby, by the way."

"Tim," I reply, taking her hand as gently as I can for fear of breaking every one of her fingers.

"You must think I'm odd, coming up to you out of the blue like this and recommending books and whatever."

"No," I lie. "I don't think you're odd at all."

"It's just I love her books so much and when I saw you pick one up …"

She stops and holds up a single boney digit, reaches into her denim jacket pocket, pulls out her iPhone and jams it against her ear.

"Hi … Yeah … OK, no problem … Sure, see you in ten minutes."

She puts the phone back and gives an apologetic shrug.

"Sorry, I gotta go. Meeting."

"No worries. It was … nice to meet you."

"You too," she says with yet another huge smile. "I hope you enjoy the book."

And with that, she dashes off as fast as her spindly legs will take her. When she has disappeared from view, I turn my attention back to the book I am holding.

I walk to the counter and make my second purchase of the day.

20

FROM: Naomi
TO: Tim
SUBJECT: Naomi says Hey!

Hey!

Sorry I haven't been in touch for a few days. Life here is super-mental at the moment, as I'm sure you can imagine!

How are you? Still bored? Did you go shopping? What did

you buy?
Have you had enough of my questions yet? Haha!

I have to tell you that I did think about what you said about smoking, but then I thought 'Fuck it! – I'm NOT quitting!' Why the hell should I make your life easier? I love that you have to go round and clean up after me! Hahaha!!!

I did take your advice about going easy on my sister though. We went out and had a great time and neither of us ended up puking or being arrested.
See? I do listen to you!

Well, the big day is finally here, sort of. Two more days and then it will all be over. To say I am going to be happy to see the end of this madness would be a huge fucking understatement. Maybe after this weekend, life will return to normal and my sister will chill the hell out for a while.

I missed my sister. It was really cool to see her again when we went out the other night. Sadly, she disappeared again the next morning to be replaced by this stressed-out doppelganger. People keep telling me she's my sister, but I know she's not.

Can I just say at this point, that I love, love, love the word doppelganger. It's just so cool.

Hey! What's your favourite word? I don't think you've ever said and I know I've never asked before. Tell me, tell me, tell me!

I seriously hope that your next email is more exciting than the last. Man, I almost fell into a coma by the end.
Of course I'm joking. But...
Tim, Tim, Tim...
Please...
GET A LIFE!!!

OK, I'm going to be super-serious now.

I miss you and hope you are OK.

Hahaha! How awesome is that?

You know what you should do? You should call up Rick or Ralph or Roger or whatever his name is. The guy who always asks if you're free and you always come up with some lame excuse why you can't go out for a drink with him.
You know, I love the excuses you give.
What's the one you always say?
Let me think...
Oh, I know!
'Sorry (enter name here), but I'm seeing Naomi tonight.'

Go on, be a devil. Go out for a beer or three. It's OK to have other friends, do you know that?

Right, time for me to say bye. I gotta go for a walk, smoke

ten cigarettes and see the nice man at the 7-11 so I can score me some mints. Then it's out for a dinner with the crazy gang.

Have fun, you!

Bye for now,

N.
xxx

19

"You are totally in love with Naomi."

Rob takes another deep gulp of his pint as I protest this is not so.

"Oh, come on," he says, coming up for air. "*Everyone* knows you have the hots for her."

"What do you mean 'everyone'?"

"People have eyes, you know. They can see how you are around her, how you look at her, talk about her …"

"Well, 'people' are wrong," I say. "We're just friends."

Rob laughs and scratches his shaved head.

"Right, friends who are going to explode if they don't

jump into bed with each other soon. Another one?"

I nod and finish what's left of my pint. Rob trundles off to the bar, whistling a certain song about love by the band, Madness.

I sigh heavily and lean back in my chair. The pub is all but empty, which suits me fine. I hate having shouted conversations in bars. Rob returns and places a fresh drink in front of me.

"Fancy a curry after this?"

"Sure, why not. I don't fancy getting hammered tonight though, I have to write an email to …"

"Let me guess." Rob grins. "Naomi?"

I sigh again and nod.

"OK now, Tim, seriously. Do you really believe you're just good friends?"

"I do," I say. "And I know that's how Naomi feels."

"How do you know?"

"I just know."

"Have you ever asked her?"

"Asked her what?"

"How she feels, if she sees you two as something more than friends?"

"No."

Rob drains half of his pint and leans towards me.

"Hand on heart, mate. You are gonna have to ask her. It's gonna drive you crazy otherwise."

"I'm not going to ask anything!" I say. "We're good friends. That's it. That's as far as it goes. I'm not going to destroy our friendship by going all weird on her. Especially as I don't know if she feels the same way."

Rob slams his hand against the table and smiles.

"And there it is. Admission. Gotcha!"

We eat in relative silence. Rob devours his chicken

madras as I wonder why I crumbled so easily. Only a week ago, I was 100 percent sure Naomi and I were simply the best of friends. Now, I've come to the realization that my feelings run much deeper.

But what about her?

Does she feel the same way?

"You're thinking about Naomi, aren't you?" says Rob.

"How do you know?"

"It's written all over your face."

"It's that obvious?"

"Yeah."

I push my plate away and reach for some liquid refreshment.

"This is a right mess," I say.

"I don't think so," says Rob, skewering a piece of my chicken with his fork. "I mean, it's better late than never, right?"

I down the remainder of my drink and signal the waiter for another round. I doubt I'll find any answers at the bottom of the next glass, but it seems like a good place to look.

We leave the restaurant and make our way to a taxi rank. A fine rain has started to fall and there is a chill in the air.

'Crazy English weather!' Naomi would say.

A black cab pulls up and Rob calls it. No problem for me, he faces a longer journey.

"You going to write to her when you get back?" he asks.

"Yeah."

"Tell her, Tim. Just bite the bullet and get it over with. What's the worst that could happen?"

"I can think of a few things."

"Ask her," he says, climbing into the cab. "Ask her before someone else does."

He shuts the door, gives me a thumbs up through the window and is gone.

'Ask her before someone else does.'

That really would be the end of my world.

I sit in front of my computer, staring at the blank email before me. I desperately try to find the right words but discover that all my vocabulary skills have left me.

After thirty minutes, every last scintilla of bravery also departs and I write to Naomi as both a coward and a liar.

18

FROM: Tim
TO: Naomi
SUBJECT: Tim goes out.

Hi Naomi,

Just a quick email as it's rather late here and I know you're busy and may not have time for my ramblings.

I took your advice and called Robert. I've actually just got back from having a few beers and a curry. Not a bad night at all.

It's raining here, as usual. How's the weather with you? I imagine the rain in HK is far more impressive than the perpetual drizzle we have here.

Oh, I bought a book today by a writer from Japan. Her name is Aurora and she writes these books about dreams and their meaning and all that kind of stuff. Have you ever heard of her?
To be honest, I don't really know why I bought it. I just picked one of her books up on a whim and someone in the shop said she was a really good writer, so I thought 'why not?'
I have a strong feeling that I've wasted my money, yet again.

I have to agree with you and say that doppelganger is a really great word. My choice would be nincompoop. It's a cracking word.

Well, time is getting on and I really ought to think about hitting the sack. Hope all is well with you and your sister's wedding turns out to be a truly wonderful occasion.

Have fun and stay happy.

Speak to you soon.
Tim.

17

FROM: Naomi
TO: Tim
SUBJECT: Naomi hits HK!

Hey,

Congratulations! That has to be one of the most boring emails I have ever had the pleasure to read. Hahaha!

Only joking, it's always great to hear from you. I consider

you to be my link to sanity amongst all this bedlam, and am always super-happy to receive your emails, even if you have fuck all to say!

Aurora? Hmm, can't say I've heard of her. Is she some kind of self-help guru or does she write stories about dreams? I'll check her out later and let you know if I think you have wasted your money.

Well, tomorrow is the big day and the craziness level has been turned up to eleven. I really shouldn't be writing to you now, as there are sooo many things to do, but I saw your mail and had to reply.
Did you hear what I said?
I said I HAD to write to you!
See how important you are to me, you nincompoop? Haha!

Anyway, this email is going to be just as short as yours, but I feel at least mine is interesting! You are gonna have to work a damn sight harder to please me, you hear?

I will email you again after the wedding with a full account of what went on and some photos, if you're a good boy. Perhaps we could talk on Skype? What do you think? Are you up for seeing and hearing me? Could you handle that? Haha!

Also, I've decided to do something crazy.
It's time that Naomi Wong bit the bullet and followed her dreams.

I'm not gonna tell you what I'm gonna do just yet, but I swear you are gonna love it!
Curious much? Hehe…

Speak soon, you big nincompoop.

N.

xxx

16

I read the email again and again. Especially the line that says 'It's time that Naomi Wong bit the bullet and followed her dreams.'

Is it coincidence she used the same phrase as Rob?

Of course it is. 'Bite the bullet' is a common saying.

I close the email and turn my computer off. Whatever she has planned will be revealed to me in due time. For now, all I can do is wait.

'I'm not gonna tell you what I'm gonna do just yet, but I swear you are gonna love it!'

Oh, Naomi. I am so much more than curious.

Rob calls me at around lunchtime to ask if I emailed Naomi.

"Yep," I say. "I emailed her."

"Did you take the bull by the horns and ask?"

"No, I didn't."

"Chicken."

"Always."

"Well, don't come crying to me when she comes back from Hong Kong and announces her engagement."

"I really don't think that's going to happen," I say. "That's too crazy, even for her."

"It will one day," says Rob. "Admit it. She's an awesome girl. She ain't gonna be single forever."

He's right, of course. She is completely awesome and I would be the world's biggest nincompoop to let her slip through my fingers.

"Anyway," says Rob. "That ain't why I'm calling. You need a job?"

"Where? At the coffee shop? With you?"

"Yeah, Andrea left, so I put a good word in for you. Fancy it?"

"Let me think about it," I say. "I was toying with the idea of doing some traveling."

"Well let me know as soon as. It'd be good if you got out of the house and earned a bit of cash of your own, instead of just sponging off your folks."

"You're too funny," I say, deadpan. "A regular comedian."

"I'm here all week," he says. "Please try the fish."

I lie on the sofa, trying my best to fight back the urge to sleep.

The movie on the TV continues to play; the actors

scream and shout as they compete with a deafening soundtrack of destruction.

Despite all this noise, all I want to do is sleep. My eyes are determined to shut, no matter how much I struggle to keep them open.

Could taking a job at the coffee shop cure me of this lethargy?

Should I call Rob now and arrange the interview?

Perhaps I should, but not now.

Now I will wave a white flag and let my eyes claim their victory.

I wake up with a start and fall from the sofa with a thud.

Scrabbling up, I run to my bedroom in search of paper and a pen. I have to write down the details of the dream before my mind presses the delete button. I grab a pen from my computer desk and write frantically on the only piece of paper I can find, the receipt for the book by Aurora.

Now there's an irony.

When I'm done, I sit down on my bed and read the scribbled details of my dream.

Naomi standing in front of a full-length mirror.

She looks at her reflection.

Her reflection steps out of the mirror.

One of them flips a coin.

The mirror shatters.

But there was something else, some detail I needed to remember. But what? What the hell was it?

Too late, the delete button has already been pressed.

Damn it.

I turn the receipt over.

Time I investigated the art of dream recovery.

Four chapters into the book and I've learned zero about remembering my dreams, but a whole load about Aurora.

Chapter One is nothing more than a two thousand word 'thank you for buying my book', the second and third chapters talk about her childhood in some place in Japan I've never heard of and the fourth briefly touches on dreams by mentioning how her grandmother would comfort her when she had nightmares as a child.

Now, I'm all for books that build up slowly, but this is a self-help book. Methinks this Aurora should cut to the chase a bit quicker.

I'm about to start Chapter Five when the phone rings.

I am not sad to be disturbed.

"Hi, Tim," says Rob. "You thought more about the job?"

"Yes, I did," I reply. "Well, for about five seconds before I fell asleep on the sofa."

"You're one lazy son of a bitch."

"Sure am."

"Well, the boss is giving me some pressure. He wants to know if you want it or not. If you don't, he's gonna put up an ad."

"The only thing I know about making coffee is instant."

"No worries, you can work on the till and clear tables. It's a piece of piss."

"Sounds awesome," I say, stifling a yawn.

"Do you want the job or are you just gonna spend your time lying on your sofa, dreaming about a girl you're too scared to ask out?"

"Get fucked."

"You might if you ask her. Now is that a 'yes'?"

I submit and say yes. Anything for a quiet life.

"Cool," says Rob. "You start tomorrow at twelve. I'll meet you at your place at ten. See you later."

"See you."

Wonderful.

I now clean tables in a coffee shop.

Somewhere in Hong Kong, I am sure Naomi Wong has just split her sides.

15

My first day at the coffee shop is all but done and, if I'm to be completely honest, it hasn't been such a bad day after all. For one thing, the coffee shop is on the edge of the city and has a steady stream of customers throughout the day, rather than being flooded at lunch and dinner.

The other thing that made my first shift enjoyable was Rob playing The Moog Cookbook CD over the shop's sound system. That album cracks me up every time. Pure genius.

"Told you this was a cool job," says Rob. "Nice and

relaxed and all the free coffee you can drink."

"You can have free coffee?" I didn't know this.

"Oh," he says, feigning mock guilt. "Didn't I tell you? Oops, my bad."

I am about to tell Rob what I think of him, when a customer enters.

"Good afternoon, welcome to …"

My customer is none other than Abby, the thin, blonde Aurora fan. She's still wearing shades, despite it being an overcast and dreary day.

"… oh, Hi." I say.

"Hi, Tim," she says, flashing another of her smiles. "I didn't know you worked here."

"Yeah, it's my first day."

"Cool."

Our conversation comes to a sudden and grinding halt right here.

I still can't help but notice how sickeningly thin she is. I want to suggest she tries one of our sandwiches or sausage rolls or both.

"So, what can I get you?"

"Oh, just a double-espresso to go, thanks."

"One double-espresso to go," I shout. Rob gives me the thumbs up and busies himself preparing Abby's beverage. After paying, she asks about the book.

"Have you started reading it yet?"

"Yeah," I say. "But I have to be honest and say I don't really rate it that much so far."

"Oh," she says, visibly disappointed. "What makes you say that?"

"It's just that I've finished Chapter Four, and she hasn't really mentioned anything about dream recall."

"Oh, I see," she says, with renewed enthusiasm. "Stick with it, Chapters Five and Six are where she introduces the concept and how to achieve it."

"OK, I guess I will read on."

"Cool."

"Double-espresso to go!" shouts Rob, a little too loudly.

"Oh, that's me," says Abby, and off she goes to fetch her dose of caffeine. She totters back, cup in hand.

"Guess I'll see you around," she says. "I usually have meetings here, so…"

"OK. Well, see you soon then."

"Sure thing. Bye."

She leaves the shop and waves as she passes the window, her huge smile still firmly in place.

"So you two know each other?" asks Rob.

"Kind of," I say, and relay the whole book-recommending incident from the other day.

"Dream recall?" asks Rob. "Don't tell me you're gonna become one of them and go all new-age on me!"

I assure Rob that won't be the case and that he can rest at ease.

"Glad to hear it," he says. "I hate the smell of patchouli oil."

"Does she come in here often?" I ask.

"Two or three times a week," he says. "Once a month, she turns up with a whole group of friends. Now, they are a *real* odd bunch."

"What do you mean?"

"The things they talk about. Fixing nightmares and other bizarre shit. Last week they were talking about sharing dreams. I tell you, they are very, very strange."

I sit at home with the receipt for Aurora's book and read my notes again and again. I still don't find any answers.

Naomi standing in front of a full-length mirror.
She looks at her reflection.
Her reflection steps out of the mirror.
One of them flips a coin.
The mirror shatters.

The missing detail nags at me like an itch between the shoulder blades, the kind that is almost impossible to scratch without assistance.

What the hell was it?

I consider reading Chapter Five but hit upon another, better idea: Why not just ask Abby and her friends? If Rob is right, they know a lot more than I do about this. Also, an answer from them would probably come a lot faster than trying to discover it for myself within Aurora's book.

Cheers, Rob. Landing me this job has made this task a lot easier.

I turn on my computer and check my email. There's nothing new from Naomi, which is no big surprise but still makes me disappointed. Happily though, I have an extremely long email from my parents, detailing their adventures in the Far East, complete with around a hundred photographs. The pang of jealousy returns as I go through the photos. It looks like my parents are having the time of their lives and what's more, Thailand looks amazing.

'*You really should have come with us,*' my mother writes.

Yes, Mom. I really think I should.

It's now three in the morning and I still can't sleep.

Every time I close my eyes, images of Naomi flipping a coin or a mirror shattering swim into view, reminding me that I failed to list the most important information when I was writing down what took place in my dream.

I turn on the bedside lamp and read the list several times before finally giving in and picking up the book. Instead of turning to Chapter Five however, I randomly turn to a page halfway through the book.

'If one were to crave for something so badly, is it possible that one could dream what one desires into existence?

There is an old saying that tells us to be careful of what we dream for. I believe this sentence to be accurate and true in every way.'

Far too deep for me, especially at this time in the morning and on zero sleep.

I close the book, place it back on the bedside table and turn off the light. Then I close my eyes and wait for Naomi to arrive.

14

FROM: Naomi
TO: Tim
SUBJECT: Naomi survives!

Hey Tim,

So, the wedding to end all weddings has finally been and
gone!
Yay!

Normal service can now be resumed.

Actually, I have to say the big day was a complete and utter disaster.

Only joking! It was really, really good. Lovely, in fact. My sister looked so beautiful and there was many a teary eye when we all saw her in her wedding dress.
Not me, you understand. I didn't cry at all and if anyone says I did then they are a big fat liar.

Hey! Can you guess who caught the bouquet? That's right, it wasn't me! Ha!

Well, my sister and her new husband are now on honeymoon in Bali. So lucky, right? I've heard that place is heaven. That's one of my dream holiday destinations, you know. That and Paris.

Speaking of dreams, I suppose I should tell you what I was going on about in my last email.

Well, like I said, I have decided to go crazy and do something I've wanted to do for ages and ages but never had the chance.

'What is it?' I hear you scream.

Well...

I'm not telling, not yet!

All I'm going to say is you're going to think I'm even cooler than you already do now and you'll find out exactly what I'm cooking up real soon.

How's your curiosity level doing? Has it gone through the roof yet?

Now don't go getting angry, you hear? I know you love me.

Best thing you can do right now is take a deep breath and count to three.

Are you ready?

OK ...

1.

2.

3.

Feeling better? Haha!

Right, I'm going to get the hell out of here before I make you blow a fuse.
Just remember, I am awesome and you know it!

Be seeing you soon,

N.
xxx

13

My internal radio has been tuned in to Shit FM all day.

The track list that has been running through my head is downright shameful. I can't bear to recall some of the crimes against modern music I've found myself whistling, or sometimes even singing along to. I blame Rob for playing his 'Hits of the Eighties and Nineties' CDs at work. 'Hits' is not the right word, although it does contain all the right letters.

When I'm not being driven slowly insane by music of pure evil, I try my absolute best to not think about the email I had from Naomi. Sadly, I fail spectacularly and focus on nothing else.

By the time the end of the shift comes, my poor brain is well and truly scrambled.

"Fancy a beer?" asks Rob as we leave the shop.

"No, I fancy several."

Six pints and a summary of Naomi's email later, Rob is finally ready to give me his brutally honest opinion.

"You ready for this?" he asks.

"Yep."

"Fly to Hong Kong, find her, tell her you love her and then fuck her brains out."

"That's your advice?" I ask.

"Damn straight," he says, and then downs the remainder of his pint.

"Genius," I say. "Pure bloody genius. Seriously, why didn't I think of that? I'm such an idiot. Thanks, Rob. You are a lifesaver."

"My pleasure," he says. "Now that's all sorted out, wanna curry?"

I must be drunk.

For one thing, I am now eating a lamb vindaloo and enjoying it.

The other thing that tells me I've had one drink too many is Rob's idea of flying to Hong Kong now seems like the perfect plan.

"You're an arsehole," I tell him.

"Takes one to know one," he replies.

"Why do you have to go and fill my head with all that shit?"

"There's nothing wrong with my taste in music …"

"I'm not talking about your bloody music!"

My speech is slurred and I'm sure a piece of lamb has fallen off my fork and onto my lap. "I'm talking about Naomi."

"You talk about nothing else." He laughs. "You're obsessed!"

"I mean flying to Hong Kong. I can't get the bloody idea out of my head. For God's sake! Why did you go and tell me that?"

"I dunno." He shrugs. "Just felt like the right thing to say."

"Well, thanks. Thanks a lot."

I push my plate away and lean back in my chair. Sure enough, there is a large chunk of curry-covered lamb on my lap.

Great.

Rob signals to the waiter to bring two more beers.

"You want to know what I really think?" he asks.

"No," I tell him. "I don't."

"I think most people who know you two are secretly waiting for the pair of you to become an item. I also reckon most people who don't really know you that well already think you are. The two of you are inseparable! Seriously, you're almost like conjoined twins!

"Honest truth, I would put money on Naomi saying 'yes' if you were to ask her out. You know what? I'm willing to do that right now."

He reaches into his trouser pockets and places a crumpled selection of notes on the table.

"How much have I got?" he mumbles to himself as he tries to make sense and order of the mess of money.

"Almost seventy," he says when he is done. "Seventy."

He pushes the pile of money towards me.

"That's how confident I am. I'll give you the money now."

"I'm not taking your money," I say.

"Either you take it or we're gonna be leaving one hell of a tip."

We sit in silence, looking at the money that sits between us.

"What if she says no?"

"She won't."

"How can you be so sure?"

"She's currently on the other side of the world, she's seeing her family for the first time in ages and there's a wedding going on. What does she do? Email you. What are you? Pen pals?"

I don't have an answer. My head is starting to spin and I'm feeling an increasing need for fresh air.

"You don't look so good," says Rob. "I reckon it's time I got you out of here."

I sit at the centre of the storm; the world around me is spinning out of control. I grip the arms of my chair for dear life and pray for calm.

I am so drunk it is untrue.

Coffee.

Coffee would be good. Coffee could save me.

If only everything would stay still long enough, I may be able to make my way to the kitchen without throwing up.

I screw my eyes shut and take several deep breaths.

One of them flips a coin.

The mirror shatters.

Please, not now…

'Now don't go getting angry, you hear? I know you love me!'

Please…

Somebody knocks on the front door.

I open my eyes. Magically, the spinning has stopped. Thanks for that. I release my grip on the chair and relax a little.

Knock, knock.

I glance at my watch. It's one o'clock in the morning.
Who the hell would be knocking at my door at one in the morning?

Knock, knock, knock.

I get to my feet and stagger towards the front door. Whoever it is outside is persistent, I'll give them that. By the time I arrive at the door, they've knocked another six times.
I undo the chain, release the catch on the lock and open the door.
"Hi, Honey! I'm home!"
It's Naomi.
Naomi Wong from Hong Kong.
"Surprise!" she says, grinning from ear to ear.
My mouth opens and shuts like a feeding catfish. Naomi starts to laugh.
"Wow, I didn't know I'd have *this* much effect on you! So, can I come in or what?"
I can't find the words. I simply stand to one side and motion for her to enter. She breezes past and disappears into the living room.

What the hell is going on?

I relock the door and follow her.

Naomi stands in the living room with her arms outstretched.

"So, do I get a hug or what?"

I shamble towards her and into her open arms. She hugs me tight and I reciprocate.

God, she feels so good. So warm. I bury my face in her hair and smell dewberry and mints. I don't want this moment to ever end.

Please, don't let this moment ever end.

"I missed you," she whispers. "I really, really missed you."

"Me too," I say, finally finding my voice. "More than I can say."

"Did you miss me like a hole in the head? That's what you said when I called you from the airport. Do you remember?"

"Yes."

"Well, did you?"

"No."

"Good, because that would suck."

I feel her embrace tighten. Her body is pressed firmly against mine.

'You're almost like conjoined twins!'

At this moment, Rob would not be far wrong.

"Do you want to know how much I missed you?" she asks. "Ask me. Ask me how much I missed you."

My mouth feels like it has been filled with chalk. I swallow painfully.

"How much did you miss me?"

"This much."

She looks up at me with those beautiful dark eyes of hers and kisses me.

Naomi Wong is kissing me.

Her soft lips brush against mine for the shortest time before she breaks away.

"You weren't expecting that, were you?" she says.

She's not wrong. I only wish it could have been a hundred times longer.

Naomi untangles herself from me and leads me by the hand towards the sofa.

"Let's sit down," she says. "I want to talk to you."

I do as ordered and take a seat beside her.

"I did a lot of thinking," she says. "I still am.

Do you remember what I wrote to you about in my last email? I said I was thinking about following my dreams and stuff, do you remember?"

"Sure," I say. *How could I forget?*

"Anyway, I said I was going to do something crazy…

"Well, this is me being crazy! You know, all I did in Hong Kong was think of you. Every single day I would be thinking 'Hmm, I wonder what Tim's doing now?' or "Does Tim miss me?' and other stuff like that. Seriously, you were like super-glued to my thoughts. Then I started to think about how long it's gonna be before you wake up and realise I really, really like you. Is it gonna be another month? A year? Never? And so I thought, should *I* do something about this? Should I be crazy and confess my love to my best friend? What if he doesn't feel the same way? What will happen then? I tell you, my brain was properly screwed up."

She stops for a moment, tucks a strand of hair behind her left ear and smiles.

"So what do you think?"

"What do I think?"

"Yeah, dummy! Do you think we should give me and you a shot?"

"A shot? Are you serious?"

Naomi howls with laughter.

"Of course I'm fucking serious! I've traveled so far to tell you how I feel and believe me when I say it wasn't easy!"

"Sorry," I say. "That was a dumb question."

"Well, you're a nincompoop, right?"

"I guess I am."

Naomi sits up, takes both of my hands in hers and looks straight into my eyes. I can't help but think she would make a first-rate hypnotist.

"Tim, I love you."

Those words sound so much better live than in my imagination.

"I love you too."

Naomi's smile has never looked more beautiful.

"But can I ask one thing?" I say.

"Sure," she replies. "What is it?"

"Are you real or just a drink-fuelled illusion?"

"Oh, I'm *very* real," she says. "And I'm gonna prove that to you in the bedroom."

12

School Of Seven Bells' second album is being played at ear-splitting volume. As alarm calls go, this one isn't so bad; I only wish the volume could be turned down. Doing my best impression of an extra from the latest zombie movie, I shuffle into the living room to find Naomi belting her heart out along to the song that's playing.

She sees me and smiles, continuing regardless. I slump onto the sofa to watch her perform. She stands in the middle of the living room, dressed only in one of my t-shirts and her underwear. I cannot help but admire her slender body as she sways slowly in time to the music. As the song comes to its end, she looks directly at me and paraphrases the lyrics.

"I love you," she says. "You know that, right?"

We eat a breakfast of ham and cheese omelets, French toast and freshly ground coffee. I comment that I didn't even know I had cheese, eggs or ham in the fridge.

"I can do magic," she says.

"Well, that breakfast was truly magical," I tell her. "Best thing I've eaten since you went to Hong Kong."

"I aim to please," she says with a wink. "And I never miss."

She finishes her coffee, stretches and yawns loudly.

"You must be jet-lagged to hell."

"Yeah." She nods. "Something like that."

"You need to get some sleep."

"Yep, think I do."

"You can stay here, if you like. No worries."

"Cheers," she says with another yawn. "What about you?"

Damn it. Now I have to tell her I work in the coffee shop.

I take a deep breath, prepare myself for a healthy dose of mockery and confess my shame.

"Cool," she says.

I almost fall off my chair.

"Cool?"

"Yep, means I get free coffee."

She gets up, walks around to me and kisses me gently on the cheek.

"You go earn some money, honey. I'm gonna go sleep."

She heads off to the bedroom and adds: "And prepare

yourself for a king-size ridiculing when you get home!"

I clear away the plates and cups from the table, deposit them in the sink and turn on the tap. As I start to wash-up, my mind turns once more to that dream.

One of them flips a coin.

Was my dream about Naomi deciding what to do about us?

Did I somehow manage to tune into her thoughts as she tried to make a decision about staying as friends or starting a relationship?

A relationship.

I'm now seeing Naomi Wong.

Who would've thought it?

I check in on Naomi to see she is dead to the world. Even when she's sleeping, she looks amazing. I tip-toe around the room, collect some clothes and leave as quietly as I can, closing the door behind me. After showering, I get dressed in the spare room and prepare to go to work. I wonder what Rob will make of my news? Knowing him, he will cut straight to the chase and ask if we have slept together yet.

"So have you two done it yet?"

I was right. "A gentleman never tells."

"Balls. You ain't no gentlemen."

"I'm not saying a word."

Rob punches the air in delight. "I fucking knew it! How many times?"

"Drop it, Rob. I'm not saying another word."

"More than once? Way to go!"

Throughout our shift, Rob squeezes as many love songs as he can into his whistling repertoire. I feel like throwing a scalding hot cappuccino in his face after his third rendition of 'I'm Getting Married in the Morning.' He finally pushes me over the edge when he starts with that terrible song from *Titanic*. In not so many words, I politely ask him to desist before I break a number of his bones.

"Chill out, will ya?" he says, trying not to laugh. "I'm just happy for you guys."

"Fine, just drop the whistling," I tell him.

"OK, no more whistling."

"Good."

"Is it OK to hum?" he asks.

"Only if you like hospital food."

We reach the end of our shift without any love ballads or physical violence. Rob asks if I fancy a pint, but I politely turn him down.

"No problems," he says. "I had a feeling I'd be back on the sub's bench now."

"Cheers for the guilt trip," I say.

Rob laughs and tells me not to worry.

"Seriously, I'm super-happy for you. About time you two got together."

I promise him we'll go for a drink after our next shift. Rob tells me not to worry.

"You have better things to do than get hammered with me!"

We leave the shop and are about to go our separate ways when Rob slaps me on the back, congratulating me on finally getting it together with Naomi.

"Real happy for you," he says. "You've made my day.

It's really great news."

"Yeah," I say. "It's hard to believe, right?"

"Not at all," he says, shaking his head. "I knew it would happen sooner or later. I had complete faith in you two."

"Cheers."

"No worries. I guess you must be pretty blown away, right? I mean, this amazing girl flew all the way back from Hong Kong just to ask you out. That's fucking amazing!"

"Yeah," I say. "You're right. It *is* amazing."

"Well, see you later. Have fun, you lucky bastard!"

Rob then dashes off in the direction of the nearest bar, leaving me alone with my thoughts as I make my way to the taxi rank.

Naomi Wong is now in my house, waiting for me to return.

Naomi Wong is now my girlfriend. She cut her visit home short, so she could ask me out.

I'm the luckiest man alive.

I only wish I could believe it.

11

I arrive home to find Naomi waiting for me with dinner prepared, a bottle of wine on ice and candles lit. The only thing missing is Barry White, but this is no bad thing. After a quick wash and change of clothes, I sit down and tuck into a steak cooked to perfection.

"Do you like it?" she asks.

"Sure," I reply. "This is wonderful. Thank you."

"My pleasure," she says. "I'm glad you like it. Really."

The food is so good it is difficult not to give it my full attention. After a few minutes of silence, I apologise to Naomi for ignoring her.

"No problem." She laughs. "Nice to see you appreciate all my hard work."

"Totally appreciate it," I say with a partially full mouth. "I never knew you could cook this well."

Naomi smiles.

"So much you don't know …"

Naomi tells me our meal is to be followed by a DVD, some romantic comedy that, supposedly, is a big hit all around the world. I confess I've never heard of it.

"People say it's real good," she says. "I thought we could watch it and totally disagree."

"Sounds like a plan to me," I say. "I love it when we rip a film apart."

"Awesome, me too."

I offer to clear away the table and wash-up, but Naomi point blank refuses to let me help.

"Sit the fuck down and shut up," she says.

I do what I am told and relax into the sofa. The combination of a day's work and a full stomach start to take their toll. I rest my eyes and hope Naomi will join me before I fall asleep.

Naomi standing in front of a full-length mirror.
She looks at her reflection.
Her reflection steps out of the mirror.
One of them flips a coin.
The mirror shatters.
One of them …

"Are you asleep?"
I open my eyes.
Naomi is sitting next to me.
"We can go to bed, if you like …"

One of them …
What?
What does one of them do?
"Are you OK?"
Naomi's left eyebrow is raised, her head to one side. This is her concerned face. I've seen it numerous times, usually before she calls me an idiot.
No.
Wait.
Something is not right.
Something is different …
But what?
Naomi leaps to her feet, grabs my hands and pulls me swiftly to my feet.
"Come on," she says, dragging me towards the stairs. "We can rip into that movie another night. Right now, you need a hot shower and then bed."
I am in no fit state to protest. Even if I was, I doubt Naomi would listen. I let her lead me up the stairs and towards the bathroom. Once we are there, she lets go of my hand, opens the door and points inside.
"In. Strip. Shower."
Once again, I follow her orders without complaint. I get undressed, moving at the speed of a man eighty years my senior. Every single inch of my body aches. My head feels as heavy as a prizewinning marrow. I stumble into the shower in the hope that scalding hot water will revive me. Sadly, it doesn't. I'm still a paid-up member of the living dead, but at least now I'm clean and smell nice.
I wrap a towel around my waist and stand in front of the steamed-up mirror. Something nags at the back of my mind, but I'm far too tired to find it. I brush my teeth and ignore my blurred reflection.

Naomi sits at the edge of my bed, scowling at the open book in her hands. Noticing I have entered the room, she looks up and smiles.

"Nice towel."

"Thanks," I say. "So glad you approve."

She holds up the book. It's the one written by Aurora. "What's this?"

"It's that book I told you about," I reply as I sit next to her. "Remember? I mentioned it in one of my emails."

She lowers the book and turns a page. Her scowl has returned.

"Right," she says. "Yes. I remember."

I watch her flick through the book, her frown very much in place.

"Do you like it?" she asks without looking up.

"I don't know. To be honest, I don't really get it."

"Good," she says, closing the book and placing it back on the bedside table. "I'm glad."

Her response is more confusing than the book in question.

"What do you mean?" I ask. "Why is that good?"

Naomi turns to me and gives me one of her sweetest smiles.

"Because it's a bad book."

Before I can pursue the conversation any further, she gets to her feet and walks towards the bedroom door.

"My turn for a shower," she says over her shoulder. "Be back in a minute."

And with that, she disappears into the bathroom.

I slump back on my bed.

"What a day," I say to the ceiling.

I close my eyes and feel sleep approaching at a rate of knots.

Still wearing my towel, I pull the duvet around me,

curl up into bed and surrender to slumber.

I am aware of someone holding me.
I can feel their naked body pressed against mine.
I can feel their heart beating.
"You know I love you," a voice whispers into my ear.
Naomi.
I want to answer, but I am unable to speak. All I can do is listen.
"I love you, Tim. I love you more than you can ever know."
I smile, or at least I think I do.
"I will love you until the end of the world."

10

I wake up to find myself alone.

Sitting on top of my alarm clock is a sheet of folded A4 paper bearing my name and multiple love hearts. I reach for the note and see it's barely seven o'clock.

Where the hell would Naomi go at such an early hour?

I read the note so I can find the answer.

Hey, Lover!

Sorry to leave without saying bye, but I didn't want to wake you. I thought you could do with your beauty sleep. Haha!

Anyway, just to let you know that I'm going home to sort out

some stuff. I'll be back some time tomorrow morning. Please have a
cup of coffee ready for me.
Will message or call you later.
I love you!

Naomi.
XXX

I lie back and wonder exactly what 'stuff' she has to
sort out. Guess I'll have to wait until tomorrow to find
out.

My alarm clock is set for seven fifteen. I see little point
in lying in bed waiting for it to start beeping. Besides, I
am now in need of the bathroom. I get out of bed, reach
for the alarm and turn it off.

It's then I notice the book by Aurora is missing.

I do a quick scan of the room but can't see it
anywhere. Although I'm half asleep, I distinctly remember
Naomi placing it next to the clock.

'… it's a bad book.'

She didn't explain what she meant by that.

Why is it bad?

Before leaving for another shift at the coffee shop, I
check around the house for the book.

It is nowhere to be found.

I suppose there's a good chance Naomi took it with
her.

But then again, why would she? Why borrow a bad
book?

Naomi Wong, you are indeed a woman of mystery.

It's a beautiful morning and no mistake; blue sky, birds

singing, the whole shebang. I am tempted to whistle as I walk, but decide against it. That would be going too far.

It really does look like Naomi did me a favor by not waking me to say goodbye. I feel totally refreshed and full of energy, which is nice for a change.

I arrive at the coffee shop to find Rob half-heartedly cleaning tables.

"Put your back into it," I tell him.

"Get fucked." Panic sweeps across his face and he scans the coffee shop to check for customers. Luckily for him, there are none.

"You and Naomi are a fine pair," I say as I make my way behind the counter. "Perfect ambassadors for the English language."

Rob smiles with genuine pride.

"I do feel that I'm a prime example of an English gentleman. Swearing one's fucking bollocks off is what England is all about, don't you know?"

Our first customer arrives, promptly putting an end to Rob's swearing marathon. And so our working day begins. Business is slow, what with it being good weather and all. Still, there are enough people in need of a caffeine fix to keep us busy.

Later, I ask Rob if he's free for a beer this evening.

"What?" says Rob in mock-horror. "Trouble in paradise *already*?"

"Nothing like that," I say. "Naomi's gone home to sort some stuff out."

"What kind of stuff?"

"I don't know. She just said 'stuff'."

"Didn't you ask her?"

"Didn't have a chance. She'd already gone when I

woke up. So, beer?"

"Sure," says Rob. "Long as you don't go all soppy on me and start pining for her. Tell you what, I'll bring some tissues just in case."

I'm about to use some of Rob's favorite words when another customer arrives. Once more, our blue language is put on hold. Perhaps it is some kind of conspiracy.

Our new customer is a middle- aged businessman in love with his phone. He never looks at me while he orders and pays, his attention is glued firmly to its screen. I go about my own business and prepare his mocha. Rob has disappeared into the backroom, presumably for a five-minute break. I finish making Phone Guy's drink and place it on the counter.

"One mocha to go."

I freeze.

Phone Guy has gone.

A woman in a white dress now stands before me.

Her arms are outstretched, her long fingers almost touch my face.

I stumble backwards and collide with a shelf of coffee mugs, sending some crashing to the floor.

The woman jerks forward, her long fingers clutching at air as she reaches for me.

Her face …

There is something very wrong with her face.

Her features are blurred. It's like she is wearing a mask

of frosted glass. The only thing I can see clearly is her hair; thick dark tendrils that seem to move of their own free will.

She starts to speak. Her voice echoes, as if coming from far away.

"You …

Are …

Mine."

Rob comes running in from the back room and asks if I'm OK.

I look at him in disbelief.

What the hell is wrong with him?

Can't he see?

It's then I realise it wasn't Rob speaking.

I turn to see Phone Guy is now giving me his complete attention.

The blurred-faced woman is nowhere to be seen.

I don't know what to say. The guy takes his coffee and beats a hasty retreat. Rob looks at me and the scene of devastation.

"What just happened?" he asks.

"I don't know. I really don't know."

9

Rob comes back to the table with his third pint of the evening. I still have half of my first, which I am sure is now flat, warm and not really worth drinking. Rob sits down heavily opposite and shakes his head.

"I don't know what to say, Tim," he says. "I mean, this is real fucking weird."

"You can say that again," I say and quickly put up my hand to stop him from doing so. "Please, don't."

Rob sinks around a quarter of his pint and looks at me for a moment. I can tell he is fighting to keep a straight face.

"I wish I never told you," I say. "I knew you'd be like this."

"I'm sorry," he says, genuinely apologetic. "It's just …"

"What?"

"You saw a ghost? In the coffee shop?"

"I never said it was a ghost."

"Well if not a ghost, then what?"

"I don't know. A lucid daydream?"

Rob finally loses control and cracks up laughing. I'm sorely tempted to throw my warm beer in his face, but I manage to stop myself.

I can't really blame him for finding my story ridiculous. If the tables were turned, perhaps I'd be the one pissing myself.

"Sorry, Tim," he says, composing himself enough to talk. "It's just I usually daydream about women like Scarlett Johansson. Personally, I'd have thought you'd be dreaming about Naomi, not a weird chick without a face."

"I *am* dreaming about Naomi," I say. "I keep having this dream, over and over again. It's driving me crazy."

Rob leans forward, his eyebrows raised.

"Care to share? I'm all ears …"

"Calm down, mate. It's nothing to do with sex."

"Shit. Oh well, tell me anyway."

And so I do.

I tell him about Naomi, the mirror and her reflection, about a coin being flipped and that one of them does something I can never remember. Rob listens in silence, occasionally sipping his pint. When I'm done, he sits back and shakes his head.

"You wanna know what I think?"

"Go ahead."

"I think Naomi Wong has blown a fuse in your head. I reckon that finally getting together with her has sent you just a tiny little bit mental. You're in shock, mate. That's what it is."

"That's your expert opinion?"

"It is. Don't worry, you don't need to pay me. This one's on the house, what with you being a friend and all."

"Can I give you some advice?"

"Sure, go for it."

"Don't give up your day job."

As usual, we end our night in an Indian restaurant. Although my mood has lifted somewhat after Doctor Rob's diagnosis, I still can't shift that spooked feeling. Rob does his level best to steer the conversation towards pastures relatively sane, but as we start dipping our papadums into mango chutney, the elastic in our conversation snaps and we hurtle back to the topic of my nervous breakdown and to Rob's most ridiculous question yet.

"Do you think you may have some sort of post-traumatic stress disorder?"

I almost choke on my appetizer.

"I'm serious," he continues. "You've been through a rough time recently."

"I've been debating whether or not to ask someone out," I reply. "Not fighting in Vietnam."

He smiles.

"Do you love the smell of Naomi Wong in the morning?"

His unexpected misquotation of *Apocalypse Now* certainly puts a smile on my face, but I have to tell him enough's enough when he starts with "The horror…the horror." Top marks to him though, as he was spot on with the voice. Sporting Marlon Brando's hairstyle gets him bonus points.

We finish our curries and order another round of drinks. I decide to head to the bathroom so I can empty my already aching bladder. The trouble with me and lager is the damn stuff seems to come out as fast as it goes down.

It's as I'm washing my hands that every bone in my body turns ice cold. Something tells me if I look up to glance in the mirror, I will see her …

The blurred-faced woman.

Moving in slow-motion, I turn off the tap and raise my head to see a severely freaked-out guy called Tim staring back at me. His eyes are wild and bloodshot, his hair looks like it hasn't seen a comb in days, and the same could be said for his chin and a razor. My reflection is only a fraction less scary than what I expected to see.

I tell the mess in the mirror he's being an idiot and turn to leave.

I turn to stare straight into what should be the face of a woman, but is only a swirling mess of colours.

The blurred-faced woman's long fingers reach out and snatch at my shirt collar and neck.

"Don't leave me," she whispers.

Her voice seems far away, but it echoes like thunder in my head.

Her voice …

I *know* that voice …

"You are mine."

As cold fingers caress my face, I am aware someone is screaming.
When I realise it is me, my grip on reality snaps and everything goes a merciful shade of black.

8

"I think you need help, mate."

We are now sitting in my living room. Every light and lamp throughout the house is switched on. I even have a torch ready in case of a power cut. Our beer has been replaced with black coffee. This time, it's me drinking the most.

On the way to my house, Rob told me he had heard a scream and that he, the manager of the restaurant and three waiters came running to the bathroom to find me lying unconscious on the floor.

"It's a good job the place didn't have a trough," he added. "Otherwise you may have come round covered in piss. Now *that* would have been embarrassing!"

I stare into my mug of cooling instant. In the blackness of my coffee, I can see a distorted reflection of myself gazing back at me. I start to wonder how long it will be before the blurred-faced woman reappears.

"Yes," I say, lifting my head to look at my friend. "I need help."

Rob first nods and then yawns.

"Sorry about that," he says. "It's been a long day."

"No shit," I reply.

"So, what do you think we should do?"

"We?" I ask.

"Sure," he says. "You think I'm just gonna sit back and do nothing while you go bat-shit crazy?"

Although his response is full of his usual levity, the seriousness of his expression is very humbling.

"Thanks," I say. "That means a lot."

"No worries." He smiles. "Besides, I don't really fancy visiting you in Arkham."

"Arkham's in America," I say. "Plus, I'm neither criminally insane or a Batman villain."

"Good point."

"Thanks."

I sip my coffee.

"Any ideas?" I ask.

Rob smiles.

"Call Ghostbusters?"

I sigh.

"Any *serious* ideas?"

Rob holds up a finger for me to wait. He pulls out his iPhone and starts tapping at its screen.

"What are you doing?" I ask.

"Sending a message."

"I can see that! *Who* are you messaging?"

Rob finishes and puts his phone on the coffee table in front of him.

"Let's see if she's up," he says.

"Who?" I ask, trying not to lose my temper and slap the answer out of him.

"Abby."

Realisation dawns on me as Rob's confident expression cracks with what looks like shame.

"Abby the dreamer?"

He nods and casts his gaze down to his phone.

"I thought you said she was a mentalist."

"Yeah, I did," he says after clearing his throat. "But …"

"But what?"

Rob's phone vibrates, saving him from my questioning, at least for now.

"You OK if I give her your address?" he asks as he reads.

I have nothing to lose by saying yes. Rob types some more and returns his mobile to its place on the table.

"Right," he says, folding his arms across his chest and giving me his sternest look. "Before you start with the Spanish inquisition, I've got all the coffee shop's regulars on my phone, so I can text them about special offers and whatnot. But yes, I did go out with her once. And no, I did *not* sleep with her, clear?"

"Clear," I say.

"Good. And yes, she is a complete mentalist."

He unfolds his arms and leans forward, his cheery face well and truly back in place.

"But right now, I'd say a mentalist like Abby could be

just the person we need."

Abby arrives at my house at one in the morning. Considering she is into dreams and their meanings, I would have thought this was eating into her quality time. Perhaps lack of sleep helps with the deciphering or something.

Then there's the whole dreaming thing. Perhaps she *is* the business when it comes to all that, but is she just as clued-up when it comes to ghostly visitations in coffee shops and Indian restaurant toilets?

Still as emaciated as ever and dressed from head to toe in black, Abby looks as if she has come straight from a funeral, possibly her own. She takes a seat at the dining table and gets straight down to business.

"So," she says in that soft voice of hers. "Rob tells me you have been …"

"Seeing ghosts," I cut in. "Yep, I have."

Abby smiles and raises an eyebrow. "Are you sure about your choice of word? Do you believe you've definitely seen a ghost?"

"What else could it be?" I ask.

"It could be any number of things. A messenger, a portent …"

"Come again?"

"A portent. A warning or sign of things to come."

"Good things or bad?"

"My understanding is they're usually bad." Abby sticks her bottom lip out. "Sorry."

I lean back in my chair. My neck, back and shoulders ache like mad. Right now a massage, a hot shower and bed would be awesome. Instead, here I am talking about ghosts and warnings of some event in the future.

'See you when the world ends.'

I squirm in my seat as a shiver runs a relay race up and down my spine.

"You OK?" asks Rob. Seems he asks me this a lot lately.

Abby leans forward, her eyes narrowed.

"Does the ghost say anything to you?" she asks.

"Yeah," I reply. "She says I'm hers and not to leave her."

"Anything else?"

"Nope."

"And it's definitely a woman?"

"Yes. Well, I'm pretty sure. I can't really see her face, to be honest. It's all kind of blurred. But the voice …"

Abby suddenly sits back in her chair, her eyes wide with either surprise or fear, I am not sure which. Her face loses what little colour it has.

"Say that again."

"Say what again?"

"About her face. Did you say it was blurred?"

I nod.

Abby lets out a low, long sigh.

"Wow," she says. "This is big."

"Big?" I ask.

"Yep. Really big."

"How so?"

Abby doesn't answer me. Instead, she fires off a fresh question.

Her words hit me like bullets.

"Have you been dreaming about mirrors?"

7

The three of us are gathered round my laptop, reading from a blog by Aurora, the Japanese dream guru. After telling Abby about my dream, she insisted we looked at Aurora's website.

"There's something you *have* to read," she had said.

I have no idea how many times the other two have read the entry, if they've read it at all. But after reaching the final line for the third time, I find myself going back to the start again.

Why I'm doing this is beyond me, for what the blog

says scares the living fuck out of me.

Dear friends and dreamers,

I write to you now to inform you of a serious matter concerning the dream world and its safety.

Recently, my dreams have been disturbed. I have been receiving messages telling me that something born from dreams has found a way to break through the barriers dividing our worlds and is now reaching out into reality.

This, of course, is most worrying.

My friends, I cannot give you any more information on this subject, as I wish for you to remain safe and do not want to have any negative influence upon any of your subconscious. However, should you see a female figure with a blurred face or find your dreams to include mirrors, remember my teachings on how to control what is around you and how to protect yourself from potential harm.

Please contact me if either of the aforementioned should come to pass.

Blessings of light, my dear friends.

Aurora.

"Looks like you need to call this Aurora," says Rob. "Seems she's the one with all the answers."

"Maybe," I say.

"Do you have her phone number?" he asks Abby. The stick insect girl laughs.

"Of course I don't! Aurora doesn't give out that kind of personal information. All I have is email."

Abby turns to look at me.

"Do you mind? If I email her, I mean."

I shake my head. "No. I don't mind at all. Go ahead."

Abby gets straight to the task at hand, her spindly fingers tapping away at the keys. I wander off into the kitchen to boil the kettle. Another coffee is well in order.

I am standing watching the kettle boil.

On the excitement scale, this ranks at about one out of ten. Still, it takes my mind off dreams of mirrors and girls without faces.

"Is this where all the cool kids hang out?"

I turn to see Rob leaning against the fridge. Again, this is much better than turning to find something that's escaped from a Japanese horror movie.

"I think this is where the crazy kids hang out."

"Same thing, ain't it?"

"Maybe. Depends on the party, I suppose."

"I was always one of the kitchen guys," says Rob, with no small amount of pride. "If you needed a drink, Rob was da man. Remember? Some of the girls at college used to call me Sir Mix-a-lot."

"Are these the girls who live in your imagination?"

"Hark who's talking," comes Rob's quick reply. The look of guilt that sweeps over his face is almost as rapid. "Sorry about that, Tim. That was bang out of order."

I tell him it's OK and not to worry. If I were in his shoes, I'd be cracking jokes too.

I mean, the whole thing is rather ridiculous, when you stop to think about it.

Just a few days ago, I realised I was in love with Naomi Wong. While I dithered around, debating whether I should ask her out, she flew back to the UK and asked me instead.

I should be on Clouds Nine, Ten and Eleven.

Instead, I'm being bothered by unfinished dreams and things that go bump in random public places. I know everything in life can't be all sunshine and that, but still.

"Earth to Planet Tim, you there?"

I shake my unwanted thoughts away and return to Rob, the kitchen and the now boiled kettle.

"Sorry I was miles away."

"Lost in the land of Wong?"

"Ah?"

"Wong, as in Naomi, your girlfriend. Remember her? Cute Chinese girl. Awesome in bed …"

I hold up my hand to stop the conversation. Rob stifles a laugh.

"She'll be here soon, right?"

I look at my watch. It's now approaching two in the morning. At some point, Naomi will return after doing whatever stuff it was she needed to do.

How am I going to explain all this to her?
Should I even try?

"Can I be honest with you, mate?" asks Rob.

"Go ahead," I say.

"This is a bit beyond me. I mean, when I saw you in the coffee shop, you scared the crap out of me. And that scream in the Indian. Jesus."

"Sorry about that."

Rob waves both hands in front of him.

"No need to apologise. Seems you are going through some freaky shit right now. It just sucks how all this kicks off now you've scored with Naomi. I mean, you finally get it on with the girl of your dreams, and then you go and lose your marbles."

I can't help but laugh, but the sound is a lot closer to a sob than I'd like.

"Don't worry, chap," Rob says, patting me on the shoulder. "I'll help you find them."

We go back into the living room to find Abby still hunched over my computer. Her black t-shirt clings to her back and I can see her spine in detail.

"Did you send Aurora the email?" I ask her.

She swivels round on my computer chair and smiles.

"Yep, all done."

"Thanks," I say. "And cheers for coming over so late."

"Not a problem. I live close anyway and wasn't asleep. Besides, the message I got from Rob was very interesting, so ..."

Interesting? I can think of quite a few other words better suited to describe my situation.

"Did you read any more of Aurora's book?" she asks, crossing her matchstick-thin legs. "You know, the one I recommended ."

"Not really," I say. "It's a bit hard to get into."

Abby nods in understanding.

"Yeah, I suppose to some her writing can be confusing at first. So, no luck in trying to remember the last part of your dream?"

I shake my head.

"Sadly no."

"Do you have it somewhere? There's a passage on protection you should read."

I shake my head a second time.

"Sorry, I've no idea where it is. I think my girlfriend took it."

"Oh, I see. Is she interested in dreams?"

Naomi's scowling face swims into view. *'It's a bad book.'*

"No," I say. "I don't think so."

"That's a shame. Maybe she could have helped you. Never mind."

She reaches into her pocket and pulls out a small velvet-looking pouch. The top is tied with golden thread. I half expect her to open it and sprinkle me with fairy dust. Instead, she offers it to me. The look on her face when I take it is like a child's on Christmas day.

"These are crystals for grounding and protection," she says, before I can ask. "Don't touch them now. There's too much alcohol and caffeine in your system. Plus your aura is soaked in negative energy. For now, put them under your pillow and try to get some good sleep. If you're feeling better tomorrow, take the crystals out, one by one, and try to feel their energies."

The bag is light in my hand, but I can feel something inside. Two or three somethings, to be precise. I put the pouch in my jeans pocket and thank her.

"Don't mention it. I hope they'll bring love and light to you."

She stretches and yawns.

"Oh, please excuse me."

"Don't worry about it. I think it's about time we called it a night."

Abby points over my shoulder and chuckles.

"I think Rob already has."

I follow Abby's finger to see Rob pole-axed on my sofa.

"Good luck waking him!"

I show Abby to the door. Outside the summer night air is surprisingly crisp.

'It's a bit nipples outside!' Naomi would say.

I thank Abby again for coming to my aid.

"Can I say it was a pleasure?" she asks. "Is that the right word?"

"If you think it is, then it is," I reply.

"Then it was a pleasure. You know, to me, this is all very exciting. When Rob messaged me, I had to come over. And then when you told us you'd been dreaming about mirrors …"

She stops in mid-sentence, perhaps because of a sudden pang of guilt at taking pleasure in what I consider to be a very fucked-up episode of the X-Files. Whatever the reason, she reaches out to take my hand.

"Don't worry. Aurora will help us. I know it."

"Let's see," I say. "Let's see."

Abby gone, I return to the living room and the slumbering Rob.

"Oi. Sleeping beauty," I say, kicking one of his feet. "Home time."

Rob promptly falls off the sofa.

"Is it kicking out time?" he groans.

"Yep. I don't want you here when Naomi arrives."

"Spoilsport."

"Ain't I?"

Rob groggily gets to his feet and picks up his jacket from the sofa.

"Don't worry," he says. "I can see myself out."

As he is walking to the door, he stops to look back at me.

"You gonna be alright?"

"Sure," I say.

"Anything weird happens, just call. OK?"

I slump down onto the sofa and give him two thumbs up.

"Not that I'll be much use, but still. Call me."

"Will do. And thanks. I owe you one."

"That, my friend, is for sure," he laughs. "Adios."

With Rob and Abby gone, the house feels a million miles wide and quiet as the proverbial morgue.

I glance over at the TV with its dead screen.

"If you're thinking of climbing out of there, just forget it," I say, closing my eyes. "I've had enough for one day, thank you very much."

6

Naomi standing in front of a full-length mirror.
    She looks at her reflection.
    Her reflection steps out of the mirror.
    One of them flips a coin.
    The mirror shatters.
    One of them picks up the coin and smiles.
    The other sinks to her knees and begins to cry.
    "No," she sobs. "He …"

I am sitting up in bed, gasping for air like I've just swum from the bottom of the ocean.

The dream …

Wait a minute …
When did I get undressed and get into bed?

"Morning, lover."

Now, I know most guys would be over the moon to wake up and find their beautiful naked girlfriend lying next to them. But after last night, I am not in the mood for surprises, no matter how gorgeous they happen to be.

"What's going on?" I shout. "How did I get here? When did you get here? How the hell did you get in?"

Amazingly, Naomi takes my onslaught of questions on the chin and laughs.

"Nice to see you too!"

Normally, one of Naomi Wong's laughs can light up my day.

Any troubles I have simply fade away when I hear that sound.

Not today.

"I don't think it's funny," I say, my voice still raised. "What the hell's going on?"

She props herself up on her left side and frowns at me.

"You know, you look so sweet when you're angry."

Before I can let loose another tirade, Naomi clamps herself to my mouth like a lamprey to a shark.

There's a fleeting second where I want to break the kiss and push her away.

But it is only a second.

We make love.
Then we have sex.

Then we fuck.

Our bodies fuse together.

No longer two people, we become a tangled collection of writhing limbs and grinding body parts.

Neither of us speaks as we caress and explore each other. The only sounds we make are sighs and groans of lustful pleasure.

At some point during the time we spend coupled together, I feel like I leave my body and float to the ceiling of my bedroom. From that vantage point, I look down at the carnal activity.

Is that really me?

Is that really us?

Naomi's movements become more and more frenzied, so much so it's hard to keep her in focus. She becomes a blur, occasionally stopping in freeze-frame. Her poses are both macabre and strangely erotic.

And then she is gone, replaced by a figure made entirely of flames.

I watch helplessly as I am burned to cinders.

. . .

My eyes snap open.

The bedroom is in darkness.

I look to the window. The curtains are slightly open, revealing a sky devoid of both stars and moon.

Like those two celestial bodies, Naomi Wong is also absent.

I try to sit up but my body refuses to move. Invisible straps prevent me leaving the bed. It takes a concerted effort to break free of these bonds, and when I eventually do make it to my feet, I am covered in a thin layer of sweat. My head feels like I've out-drunk Rob by ten pints. Everything around me is alive and swaying like the tentacles of sea anemones.

I manage to pull on my jeans and a t-shirt without falling over and then leave the darkness of my room. Outside, the hallway light is on. Although not so bright, I may as well be looking directly into the sun. I feel like my retinas have been burned beyond the hope of healing. However, after several minutes of squinting and rapid blinking, I manage to regain my vision and set off along the hallway.

I have no idea where I'm going, or what I am looking for.

Naomi, perhaps?

All I know is my feet want to take me somewhere, and I have no choice but to go along for the ride.

Halfway down the hallway, I come to the bathroom. The door is shut, but I can hear the shower running and someone humming. I recognise the tune. It's a song by Garbage, but I forget which.

Of course, the person humming is Naomi, but I walk on past and head down the stairs.

The bathroom is not my destination. My feet wish me to be somewhere else.

I descend the stairs and head towards the living room. Once there, I walk to the sofa and sit down.

There on the coffee table is my phone.

It is vibrating.

Reaching out to pick it up, I notice my hand is shaking.

I pick up the phone and accept the call.

"Hello?"

My voice sounds like it's coming from the moon.

I repeat my greeting.

"Am I speaking to Tim?"

A woman's voice. Her words are clear and spoken with perfect pronunciation. There is a trace of an accent. It reminds me of the way Naomi sounded when I first met her, before she became a fan of the more vulgar words of the English language.

"Am I speaking to Tim?" she says again.

"Yes," I tell her.

"Are you inside your house at this present moment?"

"Yeah …"

"Is anyone with you?"

"Yeah, my girlfriend's in the shower …"

"You must leave your house this instant."

"I'm sorry?"

"Please do as I say," she says, her words now filled with urgency. "Go outside. Leave the house. Do not take your girlfriend with you. Do you understand? You are not safe if you are with her."

I want to ask who I am talking to and what she is jabbering about.

Perhaps I would if things were normal.

But they are not so I do as instructed.

I walk through the living room, open the patio doors and step out into the garden.

"I'm outside," I tell the woman.

"Are you clear of the house?"

"I'm in my garden."

"Good." The relief in her voice is evident. "Walk to the furthest point possible. Put as much distance as you can between yourself and your house."

Again, I do as I'm told. I walk down the garden to my dad's tool shed and take a seat on the faded deckchair in front of it.

"OK. I'm at the other end of the garden," I report. "Now, do you mind if I ask you a few questions? Like, who the hell are you and why it's not safe to be around my girlfriend?"

"My name is Aurora. And the person in your home is not your girlfriend."

5

"I'm sorry, what did you say?"

Even a second time, her words make no sense at all. But something inside me knows what she is saying is true.

"The person in your home is not your girlfriend."

I sit on my dad's deckchair, holding the phone to my ear. Neither Aurora or I speak. Personally, I no longer have the ability to do so.

All words have left me.

"Tim, are you there?"

I nod.

"Tim?"

"Yes," I croak. "Yes. I'm here. Sorry."

"No," says Aurora. "I am sorry. I am so sorry to be the one to tell you this. But I must. It is my duty to guide and protect people. I hope you can understand this."

"I don't understand," I tell her. "I don't have a fucking clue what's happening anymore."

Never have I spoken a truer sentence.

"I understand," she says. Her voice now has comforting warmth to it. If those words were people, they would be hugging me right now.

"Tell me, please," I say. "What's happening? If that's not Naomi, then who is it?"

"I will do my best to explain," comes her reply. "Please bear with me. This may take a little time …"

"I'm aware that Abby has informed you of my connection to the world of dreams, so I will not waste precious time with a long and complicated self-introduction and get straight to the matter at hand. Several days ago while exploring the dream world, I observed a dream I found most interesting. At the time, I merely regarded what I was seeing as a portent for someone other than myself, but then I started to have the dream too.

"You know the dream I speak of, correct?"

"Yes," I say. "It starts with Naomi looking in a mirror."

"Yes. But you never remember the ending, do you?"

"No. I always forget, no matter how hard I try to remember it."

There is a slight pause at the other end of the phone. I can't say for certain, but I think I hear Aurora take a deep breath.

"Would you like to see it?" she asks.

Would I?

"How? Wouldn't I need to be asleep?"

Aurora laughs at this. If I were a poet, I would say the sound of her laughter was like a thousand tiny bells being blown by an autumn breeze.

Like Naomi's laugh, this sound brings a smile to my face.

"Just close your eyes," she says. "That's all you need to do."

Go outside, close your eyes.

It feels like I'm playing a childhood game.

"OK," I say. "My eyes are closed. Now what?"

"Now open them," says a voice to my right. "We are here."

Seconds ago, I was sitting on a deckchair facing the rear of my house. It was night time and cold.

Now, I'm standing in a small white room with a white-haired Japanese woman smiling at me.

Oddly enough, I am not fazed by this at all.

"Hello Tim," says the woman. "It's nice to meet you at last."

"Aurora?"

The person standing in front of me is a slight woman, a little shorter than Naomi and only a little heavier than Abby.

Is this the downside to dreaming? Extreme weight loss?

She is wearing what looks like a black karate suit or maybe a pair of pyjamas. Either way, these dark clothes only make her long white hair even more striking.

It is difficult to say how old Aurora is.

Fifty something?

Sixty?

The lines on her face indicate one of those figures is about right, but her eyes belong to someone decades younger.

She winks one of those youthful eyes at me and smiles. "Yes, I am Aurora. People always act so surprised when they meet me. For some reason, they always seem to be expecting someone young and vivacious. I have no idea why."

She looks around the small room, with its white walls and door, and says something to herself in Japanese. Before I can ask what she said, she switches back to English.

"Are you ready?"

"Ready for what?"

Aurora turns back to me and takes me by the hand.

"Through that door is your dream. It's a message to you from Naomi, although I didn't know that until Abby contacted me. You see, I may be able to control my own dreams, but when I wander into those of others, I am strictly an observer with limited information."

The door to the dream opens a fraction, inviting me in.

"Luckily, clever Abby gave me everything I needed to decipher this particular portent."

"You mean my phone number?"

"More than that," she chuckles. "She gave me names and a link."

"A link?"

"The pouch of crystals in your pocket. It made finding you so much easier."

I reach down and pat the left pocket of my jeans. The

crystals Abby gave me are still there.

"So," says Aurora. "Are you ready to get the answers you have been denied?"

"Not really," I admit. "But never mind, hey?"

Aurora gives my hand a gentle squeeze.

"That's the spirit, Tim."

I watch as the door slowly opens wide. I can see a room beyond, bare except for a full-length mirror leaning against a wall.

"Don't worry," she says, letting go of my hand. "You will come to no harm."

I take the compulsory deep breath and walk forward . . .

Through the door and into the dream.

4

Naomi stands in front of a full-length mirror.

She looks long and hard at her reflection. Noticing a loose strand of hair, she tucks it behind her right ear and smiles approvingly.

Her reflection steps out of the mirror and stands directly in front of her. The two Naomi's are so close their noses are almost touching.

The real Naomi reaches into the back pocket of her combat trousers and pulls out a coin. She flips it into the air. Both Naomis silently watch the coin's spinning ascent and descent.

The mirror shatters sending shards flying in all directions, but not one piece of glass hits either of the girls.

The coin falls with a tinkling noise as it lands amongst the debris.

Naomi's reflection squats down and looks at the coin to see which side it has landed on.

She picks it up and smiles.

The real Naomi sinks to her knees and lets out a heartbreaking howl of sadness and desperation.

"No," she sobs. "He is mine."

The doppelganger's smile grows wider and wider as she watches her true self slide deeper into misery.

"No," she says. "He is *mine*."

The real Naomi Wong raises her head.

Her face is blurred.

"You lost," says her reflection. "You lost him."

3

I open my eyes.

I'm once again in my back garden, sitting on a deckchair in front of my dad's tool shed.

Only now there are two chairs and I have company.

"You have a nice house," says Aurora.

"Thanks," I say. "Well, technically, it's my parents', but thanks all the same."

We sit quietly for a few moments in the dark, watching the house I call home.

"Do you think she's still in there?" I ask.

"Yes. She is inside. I am certain."

Silence falls again. This time it is loaded with an uncomfortable subtext. When I suddenly shiver, I know it's not the brisk night air.

"You now know what she is," says Aurora. "Don't you?"

"Yes," I reply. "I know."

She reaches over and holds my hand.

"So now you need to know what you must do."

"I guess so," I say. "And I'm also guessing it won't be easy, right?"

Aurora's grip tightens. "You are quite right. What you have to do will be very difficult indeed …"

The Japanese dream guru pulls no punches as she explains what I must do and what will come to pass should I fail in my mission.

What will happen to Naomi.

It is hammered home that failure is not an option.

"Do you really think I can do this?" I ask.

Nobody replies.

There is no one there.

Both Aurora and the extra deckchair have disappeared.

I think back to the night when I watched Naomi leave in the taxi.

It seems so very long ago, instead of only days.

I think back to how simple things were. No dreams or weird messages, just two friends secretly in love with each other.

How did it get so utterly fucked up?

A light goes on in an upstairs room of my house.

'Naomi' is now in my bedroom.

I have heard of having a heavy heart but until now,

have never experienced the actual feeling.

Slowly rising from the deckchair, I straighten myself up and start the short walk back to the house.

With every step, I feel something inside me edge closer to death.

By the time I have reached the back door, there is not a single shred of love left in my entire being for the girl I am about to see.

I don't bother wiping away my tears. I open the door and step inside.

2

"Hey, nincompoop!"

Not-Naomi is standing in the middle of the living room. She's wearing a pair of cut-off denim shorts and a faded NIN t-shirt that is too small for her. Her outfit shows off her body perfectly.

Perhaps that was her intention.

I close the backdoor behind me and lean against it for support.

My heart beats like it's getting ready to take off or explode.

"Where have you been?" she asks, folding her arms

and tapping her left foot. "Quick smoke behind the shed?"

"I don't smoke," I say. "Naomi does."

"Sure do," she declares proudly. "I'm a dedicated smoker, that's what I am."

"No," I say bluntly. "You are not."

"What?"

The look on her face almost makes me rethink what I'm about to do.

I've never seen her look so hurt and confused.

But almost is not enough.

I clench my fists and continue with the job at hand.

"I said *Naomi* smokes, not *you*."

The girl I am speaking to shakes her head, her arms fall limp to her sides.

"What are you talking about? I don't understand …"

"You are *not* Naomi," I say.

At this, the girl sinks to her knees, just like the real Naomi did in the dream.

"Why are you saying these things? Why?"

"Naomi is still in Hong Kong. She never came back to the UK. She never told me she loves me. We never made love. That was all you, not her."

"*I'm* Naomi!" she pleads. "I'm Naomi!"

"No," I tell her. "You're just her reflection."

After I'd seen the end of the dream, things suddenly clicked into place.

All the little clues I'd missed, those tiny signs that something wasn't right, the hints that had gone completely over my head.

Once I'd seen the entire dream, I remembered.

It was her body language.

It was all wrong.

Naomi's reflection is lying face-down on the living room floor, sobbing pitifully into the carpet.

I know it sounds wrong, but I'm so glad I can't see her face.

"Naomi comes across as this super-confident and crazy girl," I say to her reflected-self. "But she's not. Behind all the swearing and chain-smoking, she's even more insecure than I am."

I walk across the room and kneel beside the shaking mess on the floor. I have to stop myself from touching her hair.

"Now I know Naomi loves me. You're proof of that."

I stop to blink back tears and compose myself.

"All this time, me and Naomi have been too scared to admit how we feel about each other, scared that if we say anything we would destroy our friendship. Stupid, isn't it? Why didn't either of us have the balls to say something? I mean, it's not like we didn't have the opportunity, right?"

The girl on the floor lets out a long haunting groan. Thankfully, most of the sound is muffled by the carpet.

"Perhaps all this is my fault. If I'd been a man, I would have asked her out ages ago. Sad thing is, I'm a complete chicken. If only I'd fucking known what was going on inside her head and heart, I could have stopped this from happening."

Before I can say another word, the floodgates open. Tears run down my face in rivers.

The anger I feel towards myself is beyond measure.

"Naomi's love for me caused a war," I say. "A war between her true self and what she pretends to be."

The girl on the floor falls quiet. Every now and again, she twitches ever so slightly.

"A full-blown battle between her insecurity and her

confidence."

The twitching stops.

Not-Naomi now lies perfectly still and quiet as death.

"And you won."

Aurora told me if I wanted to save my Naomi, I would have to kill her projected confidence.

To do this, all I would have to do is deny her.

To tell her the love between us was dead.

Aurora warned me that Naomi's reflection may fight back.

She was not wrong.

Not-Naomi moves at a speed that is impossible for my eyes and brain to process.

One second, she is face-down on the floor. The next, she is not only on her feet but has me around the neck with both hands and is slamming me against the wall.

"Yes," she screams into my face. "I won. I. Fucking. Won."

Should I ever see my Naomi again, I pray to all known deities that I never ever see her like this.

Her face is streaked with tears. Strands of her black hair stick to her forehead and cheeks. The lips that kissed and explored my body are now pulled back, displaying her teeth in a feral snarl.

But it's her eyes that will haunt me.

There is nothing in those twin black pools but hate.

Nothing remotely human.

Nothing Naomi.

I am slammed against the patio doors. I hear glass crack and shatter.

Then I'm on the floor, the breath knocked out of me. Pinned down by something not from dreams, but the king of all nightmares.

"Yes!" Not-Naomi hisses. "I won! Do you really think *she* would ever tell you how she feels? Do you really think she'd admit she loves you? Do you think she'd ever kiss you like I do? Fuck you like I do? Do you?"

The hands around my throat tighten, her nails dig into my neck.

"No! She'd never do any of that. Because she's TOO FUCKING SCARED!"

My vision is filled with dancing lights. Not-Naomi continues to scream and shout as she strangles me.

Her face becomes more and more distorted.

Less and less Naomi.

"I don't love you."

How I manage to say those four words is a miracle, considering the vice-like grip that's crushing my windpipe.

But say them I do.

"I don't love you."

Suddenly, I can breathe again. Not-Naomi is no longer holding me down.

I take in several deep lungfuls of air and close my eyes. My entire body is numb.

"What did you say?"

I want to open my eyes but I can't. It's like they're super-glued.

"What did you say?"

The words are whispered into my left ear. Not-Naomi's hair tickles my nose. I can feel her hand pressed against my chest. My heart pounds against her palm.

I swallow painfully and answer her question.

"I do not love you."

There follows a moment or two of sublime

weightlessness as I take to the air once more. Sadly, this feeling is short-lived and replaced with a burning agony when I smash into the wall again.

I slide to the floor in a broken heap.

Man, is this gonna hurt in the morning.

My head pounds out a drum track that would make Liam from The Prodigy sick with envy. Over the top of that, comes the soundtrack of my living room being destroyed.

More glass shatters. Objects thump and thud around me. I hear something buzz and spark, probably the death throes of the TV.

But above all this, there is another sound.

One word, repeated again and again and again.

A mantra of pure anguish.

"NO. NO. NO. NO. NO. NO. NO. NO. NO. NO. NO!"

And then …

Silence.

I flinch as Not-Naomi cradles my face in her hands. The tip of her nose touches mine. I feel her hot tears fall onto my cheeks like summer rain.

"Please," she whispers. "Don't leave me. I can give you everything you've ever wanted. Everything you've ever dreamed of. Please …

"I love you, Tim. Please tell me you love me. I'll die without your love. Please, Tim. Please."

Somewhere in Hong Kong, there is half a girl.

Her confidence found a way to separate itself from her and projected itself into the real world.

Because of both her love for me and her fear of losing what we have, she ripped herself in two.

Somewhere in Hong Kong, there is a girl who is

fading away.

A girl who is slowly slipping out of focus.

I cannot let this happen.

"I love a girl called Naomi Wong. Not you."

Seconds pass.

I wait.

Any moment now, I'm going to be hurled around the room like a toy or I'll be throttled to death.

The seconds become minutes.

Nothing happens.

I open my eyes to find the living room in darkness.

Even without light, I can see the room has been totalled.

And there's something else I can see.

Not-Naomi has gone.

I lean my head against the wall and smile.

"I love you, Naomi."

1

When the police arrived and found their way in through the broken back door, I explained to them how I had disturbed a burglar and he became extremely violent.

Apparently, a house in a neighboring street had been broken into and trashed that same night, so my story was bought and I was shipped off to hospital.

Crazily enough, aside from two broken ribs and a dislocated shoulder, the rest of my injuries amounted to nothing more than cuts, bruises and two black eyes.

Telling Rob and Abby the events of that night was easier than I thought it would be.

"So," said Rob. "Let me get this straight. The Naomi that came back to the UK was really an astral projection of her confidence and desire and the blurred-faced ghost thing was the real Naomi asking you for help. Am I right?"

How he got that after hearing the explanation once will forever be a mystery.

I guess there is much more to Rob than meets the eye and a hell of a lot more than people give him credit for.

The difficult task of explaining to my parents about their living room was made a lot easier by the generous kindness of an unknown benefactor.

Answering a knock at the door, I was greeted by a group of men in overalls unloading a plethora of boxes from a large black van.

After confirming my name and the address, the men then proceeded into my house and started unpacking their boxes.

An hour later, my folks' living room had a new patio door, new shelves and bookcases, replacement vases and ornaments, light fittings and a brand spanking new TV.

Then the men left.

I didn't ask too many questions. I chose to let them get on with their job. After everything I'd been through, a visit by a band of mysterious good Samaritans was a welcome change.

My parents eventually returned home from Asia, suntanned and invigorated by their trip. Of course, I had to explain about the 'burglary', in case the police popped in to do a follow-up or something while I was out.

My dad looked around the living room and shrugged.

"You know, I wouldn't have noticed if you hadn't told

me."

Asia did a good job of mellowing my Dad out.

I call Naomi again and again.

She never answers.

I send emails that receive no reply.

The pain is more than anything inflicted by Naomi's reflection.

I think about calling Aurora and asking if she can help. But I am too scared of what she might say.

And then, one evening, I receive a call from Naomi's sister.

Exactly one month after Naomi left for Hong Kong, I book a flight and follow in her footsteps.

0

Jessica picks me up from Hong Kong International Airport. Other than her glasses and longer hair, she's the spitting image of Naomi.

"Nice to meet you," she says as we shake hands. "Thank you so much for coming."

I tell her it's not a problem and thank her for getting in touch.

"I would have got in touch a lot sooner," she says, half smiling. "If my sister hadn't done such a good job of keeping you a secret."

"So how did you find out about me then?" I ask. "Did

she eventually tell you?"

Jessica shakes her head. "I saw all your missed calls on her phone. So I hacked into her email and read all about you."

"You hacked her email account?"

Naomi's sister gives me a mischievous wink. There is not a single trace of guilt on her face.

"It's easy when you know how she thinks. All her passwords are the same. She's so predictable. Plus I caught her emailing you several times. When I asked who she was writing to and why she didn't use Skype, she got all defensive."

Jessica does an absolutely perfect impression of her younger sister. I can't help but laugh.

"What? And have you and Mum spying on me? No fucking way!"

We get into Jessica's car and start our drive through Hong Kong.

On any other occasion, I would be glued to my window, busy taking in my new surroundings, marveling at this modern but ancient place. Today, all my attention is focused on Naomi's sister and what she has to say.

"I was in Bali at the time on my honeymoon," she says. I interrupt to congratulate her. She smiles and nods thanks before continuing. "I get a phone call from our mum. She tells me that something has happened to Naomi. I ask her what, but my mum can't explain. She just keeps telling me that something has happened to her. That something is wrong."

Jessica stops and laughs. The sound holds a certain amount of sarcasm.

"You always hear stories of family keeping bad news a secret from people who are on holiday, only telling them when they return home. Well, not our mother!"

She sighs to herself and shakes her head slightly.

"Anyway, we cut our honeymoon short by ten days and flew back home. There was no other option. She's my sister. I know she would do the same if she were in my position."

Of course, I already know what happened to Naomi. I know better than her sister does.

But I have to ask.

"It's hard to explain," she says. "The doctor's closest diagnosis is Naomi's suffered a nervous breakdown, but no one can say for certain what caused it. When I first saw her …"

Jessica exhales deeply.

"What was she like?" she asks. "In England, I mean. What was she like?"

"Honestly?"

"Yes."

"She was a foul-mouthed smoking machine who liked to talk complete rubbish."

Jessica snorts with laughter. "So you liked her a lot?"

"Yeah," I say. "I still do."

We drive in silence for a while. Much to my surprise, the landscape is no longer a fusion of a futuristic city and ancient temples. It's nothing but green hills with clusters of small houses scattered here and there.

"Naomi's living with me and my husband," Jessica says. "It's quiet here and the air is good. We thought it may help with her recovery, but so far …"

"No change?"

She shakes her head.

"You know what it's like?" she says. "It's as if all her

confidence has been drained. I know that sounds crazy, but that's how I feel when I look at her. Half of her is missing. All her vitality and will has been taken away. She's just an echo that's slowly fading and will soon disappear."

The mountain of guilt I feel makes the hills we are driving past seem tiny .

We arrive at Jessica's home, a three-story place surrounded by tall green trees. I can imagine it cost quite a lot. I am tempted to ask what she and her husband do for a living, but decide against it.

She leads me around the left of the house and through a small gate.

"This way," she says. "She'll be in the back garden."

I follow Jessica into a garden that would make my parents die of jealousy. I've never seen so many flowers in one place, except for when I was a kid and was dragged to nurseries every Sunday afternoon after lunch.

But it's not the flowers and the beauty of nature that catch my eye.

Sitting on a white picnic chair in the middle of the garden is Naomi.

I start walking towards her.

My heart is racing and my eyes mist over.

"Get a grip," I tell myself. "Don't lose it now."

I make it to Naomi without crumbling and sit down on the grass facing her.

Neither of us speaks.

It's hard to say whether Naomi even knows I'm here. Her expression doesn't change. She looks deep in thought, pondering something that requires every last iota of her concentration. Her eyes look straight through me, focused on a point somewhere in the distance. Somewhere far from here.

I, however, can only look at the girl before me.

My heart doesn't only break when I look at her.

It shatters.

Her hair is longer than last time I saw her, which comes as no surprise. She's also lost some weight. Nothing too shocking there.

What chokes me up is her eyes.

When I look into her eyes, I can't see Naomi at all.

The spark has gone.

Dear God, what have I done to her?

Does she have any idea what has happened?

I can no longer control myself. The guilt and sadness come flooding out of me. I cry until there is not a single tear left in me.

"Has the world ended?"

Her words are said so softly, they are barely audible.

"Has it? Has the world ended?"

Her expression has not changed. When she speaks, I can hardly see her mouth move. It's like she's been transformed into a ventriloquist's doll.

"No," I say, wiping my tears away on the back of my arm. "No. it hasn't. The world is still very much alive and kicking."

"Then why does it feel like it has?"

A single drop of salt water makes its way from the corner of her right eye to the tip of her nose. I watch as it falls into her lap.

I reach across and take both of her hands in mine. Her skin is so cold.

"This isn't the end," I tell her. "We still have a long time before the apocalypse is due."

"Do you promise?"

"I promise."

A light breeze brushes its way through the trees and flowers, before gently tugging at my clothes. I suddenly feel very tired. My eyes close of their own free will.

Sleep is almost upon me when Naomi asks a question.

"If the world was about to end, what would you do?"

I smile.

"Exactly what I'm doing now," I say. "I'd spend it with you."

END.

About the Author

Simon Paul Wilson is a U.K. based writer of horror, cyberpunk, and magic realism. He is the author of *GhostCityGirl* and is currently working on its sequel, as well as other things. When not writing, Simon listens to post and prog rock at a very loud volume. He also plays a mean air-bass.

Special Thanks

My deepest thanks to all the lovely people who support my writing endeavours. You know who you are. Big love to you all.

Also, my sincerest thanks to You, the person holding this book. Thank you so much for reading; it truly means a lot to me.